Thank You, Mr. Panda

Originally published in Great Britain by Hodder Children's Books, an imprint of Hachette Children's Group

ISBN 978-1-338-54740-5

12 11 10 9 8 7 6 5 4 3 2 1   19 20 21 22 23 24

Printed in the U.S.A.   14

This edition first printing, January 2019

Thank You,
Mr. Panda

Steve Antony

SCHOLASTIC INC.

 Who are all
the presents
for, Mr. Panda?

My friends.

This is for Mouse.

A present for
me, Mr. Panda?

It's the thought that counts.

But it's too big.

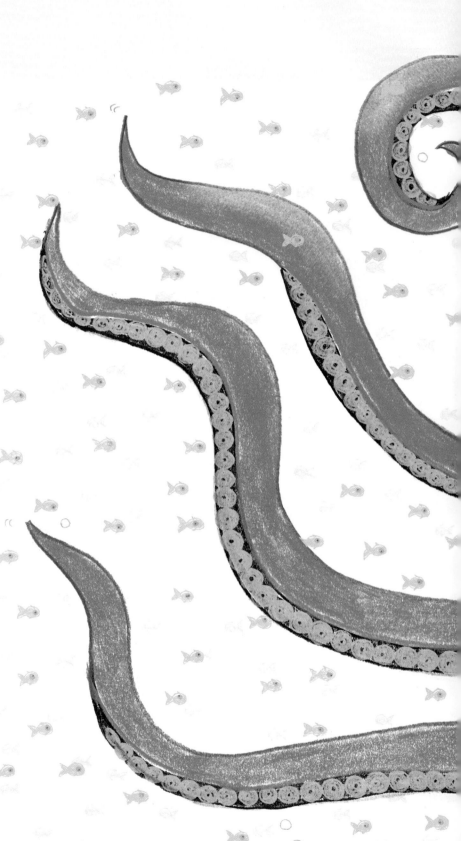

This is for Octopus.

A gift for me,
Mr. Panda?

But I have eight legs.

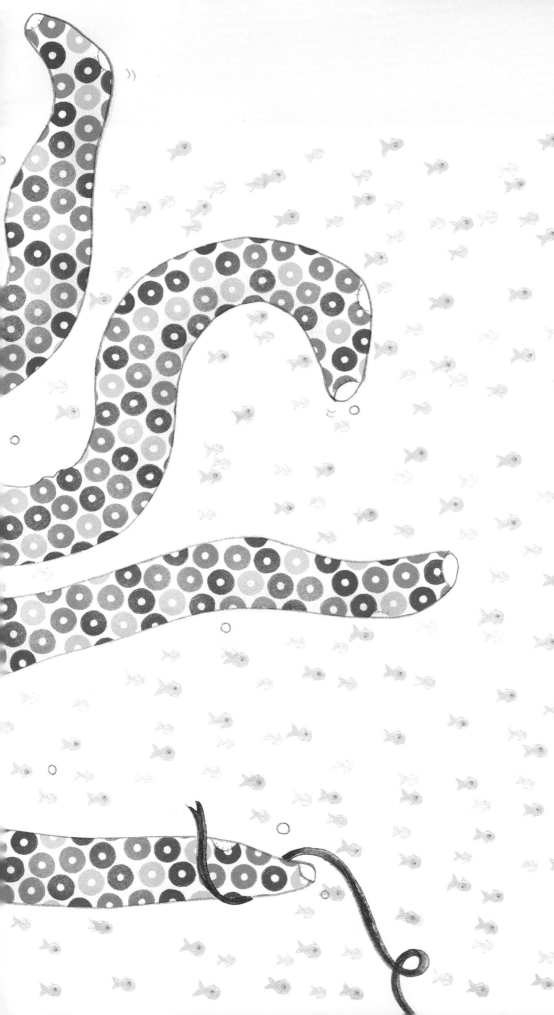

It's the thought that counts.

This is for Elephant.

I will open it later.

And this is for
Mountain Goat.

Something for me, Mr. Panda?

But it's too long.

It's the thought that counts.

Who is the
last present
for, Mr. Panda?

It's for you.

Thank you, Mr. Panda!

You're welcome,
but remember . . .

. . . it's the thought that counts.

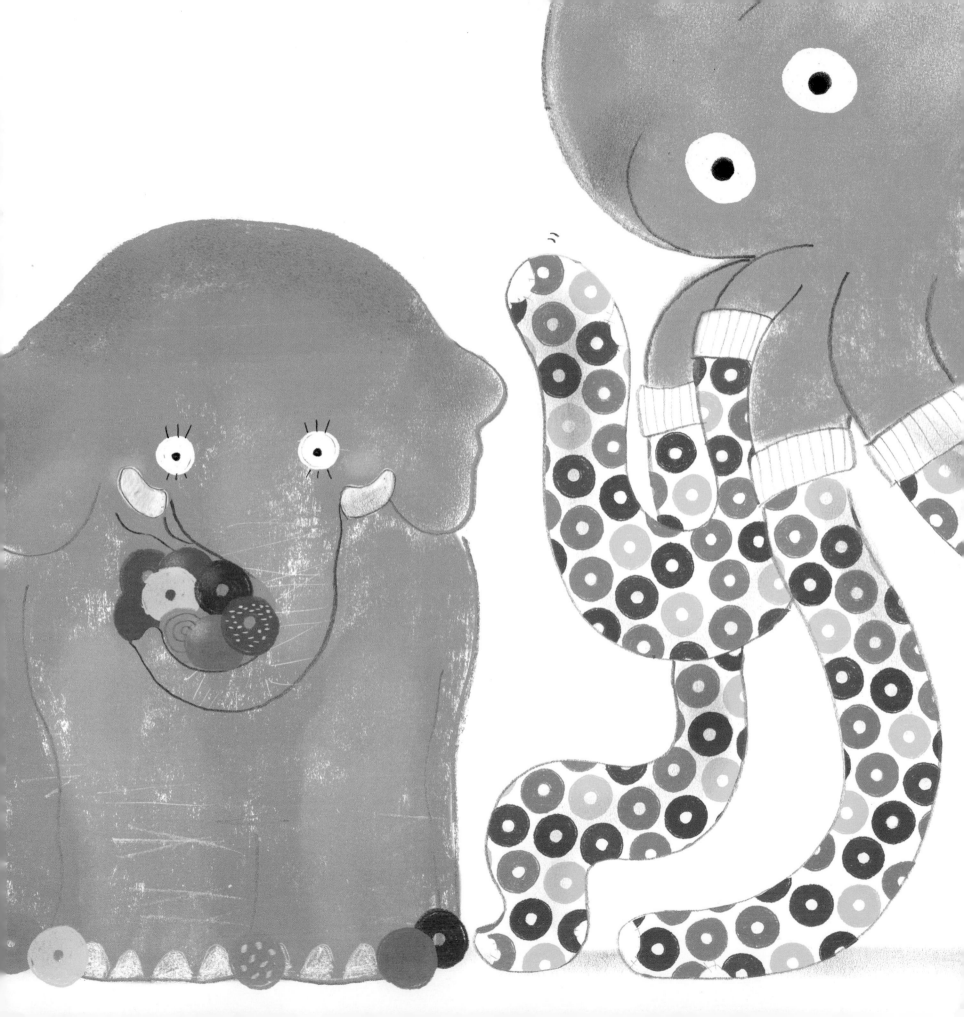